The Family of Ree

By
Scott E. Sutton

www.ScottESutton.com

The Family of Ree™ Adventures is a trademark of Scott E. Sutton. Published by Sutton Studios, Inc.
ISBN 978-0-9851061-1-9. Design and layout by Susie Sutton. Printed in China.

Welcome to Ree

I'm going to tell you about a place
Way far out in outer space.
A world whose colors are blue and green,
Sort of like pictures of Earth you've seen.

We call this place the World of Ree
And it is home for my friends and me.
It has two moons up in the sky.
When you can't see one, the other goes by.

It's a magical world that is covered with trees
And twenty-plus-two freshwater seas.
There are lots of great people that live in this place,
In this world far out in outer space,

Like Flying Floogies as small as a mouse,
Or Beasties and Dragons as big as a house.
The world is run by Wizards and Trees,
And Sea Queens, too, who care for the seas.

The work we do is too much for one,
So we have assistants, to help get it done.
I am a Wizard. My name is Dundee,
And my helper, Jeeter, is here with me.

We're going to take you through this book,
To the World of Ree and take a look.
You do not have to leave your room.
Use your imagination … take off and go ZOOM!

Ree's Talking Trees

The Trees you see
That live on Ree,
Will be a big surprise.
When you get close
To look at one
You won't believe your eyes.

The Trees you see that live on Ree,
Are not Earth trees, I say.
'Cause they have faces like we do
And like to talk all day.

The Talking Trees that live on Ree
Work with the Wizards closely,
Caring for this world of ours
But soaking up sunshine, mostly.

The Talking Trees that live on Ree
Have help to get things done.
From people we call "Beebees",
Working hard and having fun.

Beebees in the Trees

These little round people are Beebees, you know.
The size of a melon is as big as they grow.
They live in the Trees and keep them quite clean.
They're the very best helpers a Tree's ever seen.

Each one of Ree's Trees,
Wherever they sit,
Have just one Beebee
To help them, that's it.

When a Tree needs a Beebee
To have around,
The Tree drops an acorn
Onto the ground.

And before you know it,
From out of the top
Of that big acorn,
A Beebee will pop!

They goof up sometimes, like me and you.
But without the Beebees what would the Trees do?
When Beebees grow up they get to be
One of the Erfs that live here on Ree.

Little Green People

These little green people
Are called the Erfs.
You see by their looks,
They're not from Earth.

These little green people
Have very big feet.
They have pointy ears, too,
And they sure love to eat.

This little green person,
Whose name is Jeeter,
Works very hard
And makes things neater.

He may look funny
But he is no fool.
To be a smart Erf
He goes to Erf School.

He likes to go hiking,
No matter how rough.
He's a curious Erf
And likes to see stuff.

These little green people are important, you see.
They help us take care of the World of Ree.
One thing about them that's very well known …
Erfs become Wizards when they are full grown.

We Are Wizards

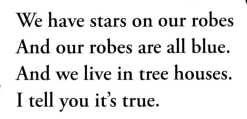

We are Wizards.
Did you know that?
We are magical people
From our shoes to our hat.

We have stars on our robes
And our robes are all blue.
And we live in tree houses.
I tell you it's true.

We are all quite good
With the magic we use.
We can fly or float
To wherever we choose.

We care for things,
That live on the land,
With the help of the Erfs
Who give us a hand.

We Wizards and Erfs
Are busy all day.
Ree is a nice place
And we keep it that way.

When a Wizard gets old
On the World of Ree,
Then he will become
A Talking Tree.

Gorbees Are Gorbees

These little plumpy porpoises
Swimming in the sea,
Aren't little plumpy porpoises,
Not on the World of Ree.

These little plumpy porpoises
That swim and dive with ease,
Aren't porpoises at all, you see.
On Ree they're called "Gorbees".

These little plumpy porpoises,
The way they come to be
Is a Tree will drop an acorn
Into the deep blue sea.

These little plumpy porpoises
Will, in a day or two,
Pop out of the Tree's acorn
And swim the ocean blue.

These little plumpy porpoises
Are the Beebees of the sea,
Helping out the Sea Queens
Wherever they may be.

These little plumpy porpoises
Will someday grow to be
One of the Sea Princesses
That help the Queens of Ree.

Sea Princesses

Sea Princesses help
Sea Queens get through
All of the sea work
They have to do.

Like watching Sea Beasties
And all kinds of fishes,
And other sea people
Like Gorbees and Splishes.

They breathe on the land
And under the sea.
They talk to the fishes
Like you talk to me.

They're a little bit taller
Than the size of an Erf.
They can ride Sea Beasties
And swim in the surf.

All Sea Princesses
Have good Gorbee buddies.
And each Sea Princess
Goes to school and she studies.

Each Sea Princess
Will grow up to be
One of Ree's Sea Queens,
Who cares for the sea.

Sea Queens of Ree

On Ree there are islands
Way out in the water
Where the weather is nice
And a little bit hotter.

The islands are covered
With Trees and flowers
That smell so good
You could smell them for hours.

These Tree covered islands
Have beaches of sand,
And each group of islands
Is a Sea Queen land.

The Sea Queens take care
Of all of Ree's seas,
And they work together
With the Wizards and Trees.

Who helps them out
With this sea watching chore?
Sea Princesses do.
That's what they're here for.

They travel the seas at a very quick pace,
Riding Sea Beasties all over the place.
When Sea Queens get old, then where do they go?
That's one thing about them we don't really know.

Sea Beasties, Sea Beasties

Sea Beasties, Sea Beasties
How big do they grow?
How deep can they swim?
We don't really know.

Sea Beasties, Sea Beasties
Their colors are bright.
If you stand by the sea,
You might see one at night.

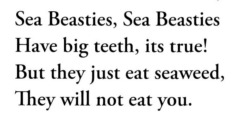

Sea Beasties, Sea Beasties
Have big teeth, its true!
But they just eat seaweed,
They will not eat you.

Sea Beasties, Sea Beasties
Swim quickly, you know,
And Sea Queens will ride them
Where they need to go.

Sea Beasties, Sea Beasties
Sometimes late at night
You might hear one singing,
If the moon is just right.

Beware … Dragon!

Here comes a big Dragon
Through the green Trees.
The ground rumbles
Whenever they walk.

These Dragons might do
Whatever they please.
They roar loudly
Whenever they talk.

They can crumble big rocks
With a swish of their tail
They can climb up tall mountains
… No sweat.

But the one thing that makes
A Dragon turn pale
Is to get his four
Dragon feet wet.

They look a bit scary, but they're not really bad.
We Wizards keep them in line.
Making sure the Dragons don't make anyone sad,
And posting … "Beware Dragon!" signs.

Long-Legged Ploots ... with Very Long Snoots

There is nothing as tall as Long-Legged Ploots.
There's nothing as long as Ploots' long snoots.
Their feet are gigantic,
Their smiles ... so romantic,
You might even say ... "They are cute!"

When they drink water
They can drink a whole lake.
If you see a dry lake,
It's Ploots, no mistake.

They eat veggies, too,
Much more than we do.
To them veggies
Are like chocolate cake.

The way that they get more Ploots around
Is when a Moonflower falls to the ground,
In less than one hour,
From out of that flower,
A new baby Ploot will then be found.

Snow Pookas

There's a part of Ree
Where snow fills the sky,
Where the Trees are so old
They've grown very high.

There's a group of people
Who live up there,
Deep in the forests,
In the snow and cold air.

They have a small tail
Behind on their seat
And three, not two,
Big snow - walking feet.

They look just like
Big fuzzy white pillows,
But "Snow Pookas" are what
We call these fellows.

They live way up north
And help out the Trees.
It's too cold for Beebees
Because they would freeze.

To find the Snow Pookas
In Northern Ree,
Look for lots of white snow
And that's where they'll be.

Flipping Floating Flying Floogies

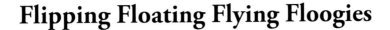

The Flipping Floating Flying Floogies
Fly flapping through the trees.
The Flipping Floating Flying Floogies
Like flying by the sea.

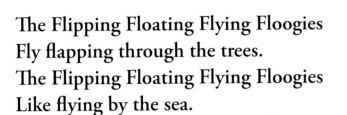

The Flipping Floating Flying Floogies
Like flying best at night.
The Flipping Floating Flying Floogies
Like the bright moonlight.

The Flipping Floating Flying Floogies,
Are flying puffs with wings.
The Flipping Floating Flying Floogies
Are funny flying things.

Splashing Splishes

These sea people here
Are called Splashing Splishes.
They look like a mix
Of flowers and fishes.

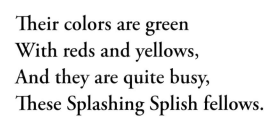

Their colors are green
With reds and yellows,
And they are quite busy,
These Splashing Splish fellows.

They smile a lot, too,
And it is quite true,
When you see a Splish smile
You cannot feel blue.

There are so many Splishes
In the seas of Ree,
That if all of them swam
Past you and me,

It would take us all
Two hundred years
To count each one
Of the Splishes' two ears.

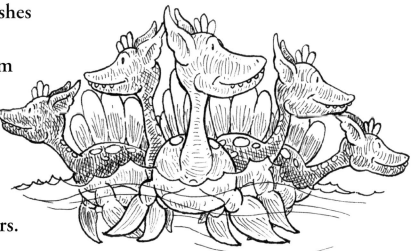

The Facts about Muppies

No, these aren't puppies.
Yes, these are Muppies.
No, they're not skuzzy.
Yes, fat and fuzzy.

Yes, they do play.
Yes, most of the day.
No, they're not scary,
But yes, very hairy.

Yes, they eat weeds,
And yes, they eat seeds.
No, they don't fly.
Yes, sometimes they try.

No, they're not slim,
And yes, they can swim.
But no, they're not guppies.
So yes, these are Muppies.

Mushroom People, I think

There are houses on Ree
That go underground.
If you are near them
And you look around,

You might see some Mushrooms.
You might see a bunch,
Much bigger than the ones
That you eat for lunch.

You will be surprised
When you see one walk.
And surprised even more
When you hear one talk.

What sort of Mushrooms
Could these be,
That have arms and legs
And eyes to see?

These aren't the Mushrooms
That you would know.
Are they Mushroom people?
Yes, I think so.

These people are farmers,
Growing veggies all day.
They keep some to eat
And trade some away.

Ride the Giant Snails

Riding Giant Snails
Is easy to do.
Anyone can do it.
Yes, even you.

If you think these Snails
Have "get up and go",
You'll be disappointed
'Cause they move very slow.

After a while
The ride gets boring.
Stay on too long
And soon you'll be snoring.

So, riding Giant Snails
Can be fun to do,
If moving real slow
Is fun for you.

Funny Looking Islands

If we look at the lakes,
On the World of Ree,
Up in the mountains
Or down by the sea,

You may see things floating
In the water out there,
Bobbing around
Without any care.

"Funny looking islands,"
You might say,
Until you see one of them
Swimming away!

And you will see
You've made a mistake,
When the "funny looking island"
Climbs out of the lake!

No, they're not islands.
They look like big frogs,
But frogs they are not,
We just call them Pogs!

Bobbing Bungalla Bingallees

The Bungalla Bingallees
Bob about happily,
All over the seas of Ree.

The Bungalla Bingallees
Like to bob comfortably
Under the shade of a tree.

The Bungalla Bingallees
Are a bobbing variety
Of fish that live in the sea.

The Bungalla Bingallees
Bob about endlessly
'Til they're hungry as they can be,

Then the Bungalla Bingallees
Dive under quickly
To eat food under the sea.

The Bungalla Bingallees
Then float back up happily
And keep bobbing … naturally!

The Bugamites

Many thousands of years ago,
Exactly when, we don't really know,
Our world was attacked by a very bad bunch
Of bug-looking Bugamites that came to munch.

They ate plants
And trees of every kind.
They tried to eat up
All they could find.

But the plants and trees
Are important to Ree
And without the plants
Life could not be.

Where did they come from?
We do not know.
But one thing was sure,
They sure had to go!

Bugamites and Dandyboo Flowers

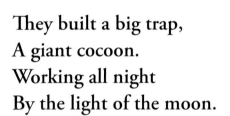

Ree was in trouble, the worst trouble ever.
They needed a plan and it had to be clever.
So, they thought of a plan. It took many hours.
They found out these bugs liked Dandyboo Flowers.

They built a big trap,
A giant cocoon.
Working all night
By the light of the moon.

When the trap was finished,
All the people on Ree
Picked every Dandyboo Flower
That they could see.

They picked them all
From wherever they grew,
And filled the cocoon
Until they were through.

The Powers of the Flowers

The Bugamites came.
They were under the powers
Of the sweet smelling smell
Of the Dandyboo Flowers.

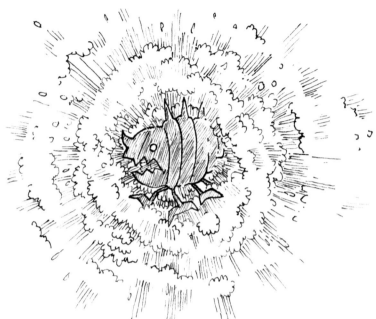

They followed the smell
Into the cocoon,
And were all locked inside
By the late afternoon.

The Sea Queens and Wizards
Raised up their hands.
They were using some magic.
It was part of their plans.

Even though the cocoon
Was a very large size,
With the magic they used
They still made it rise.

Just then it exploded,
Like this ... KABLOOO!
Was that the end?
Oh no, they weren't through.

They changed those bugs,
Right there in the skies,
From Bugamites
Into ... Butterflies.

Bugamites to Butterflies

Were the Butterflies bad?
Oh no, they were good.
They took care of the plants
Like a Butterfly should.

Are they still here?
Did they all fly away?
No, all the Butterflies
Are still here today.

From that time on in good or bad weather,
The people of Ree all worked together,
Making sure there were healthy plants and trees
And clean water, too, in the lakes and seas.

So take care of the world
Where you belong,
After all, it is
What you're standing on.

MAP OF THE WORLD OF REE

MENJEE,
THE
SMALL MOON

NORTH REE

NORTH
SEA

TRAZINO
SEA

SUNSET
SEA

SUNRISE
SEA

DUNDEE'S
TREE
HOUSE

SOUTH
SEA

SOUTH REE

MAZOON,
THE
BIG MOON

MAP DRAWN BY
THE WIZARD DUNDEE